SANTA'S express reindeer

by Bryan Rucklos

Illustrated by Roksolana Panchyshyn

This book is dedicated to those who believe...

ISBN:
ISBN-13: 978-1512201192

Long ago in the frigid North Pole, there lived nine reindeer. Though these were no ordinary reindeer.

Santa picked these nine out of all the others for a very important job. He needed them to pull his sleigh on the night of Christmas Eve.

There was Dasher, Dancer,
Prancer, Vixen, Comet, Cupid, Donner, Blitzen,
and the most important reindeer of all Sonic.

Sonic was very special.
He was the fastest and strongest of all and
that is why Santa chose him as his lead reindeer.

Until one foggy Christmas Eve when Sonic's speed and strength were no match for Old Man Winter's fog. Rudolph's red nose was the only thing that allowed Santa to see in the gloomy air.

It saddened Santa, but he needed Rudolph so he could deliver the presents on time. Sonic was no longer the lead reindeer as he watched Santa fly off into the stormy night.

Sonic had to find a new reindeer job. At first he tried being a reindeer taxi for elves. Then he became a newspaper delivery reindeer.

Sonic even helped stock Santa's factory with toy supplies. However, none of these jobs made him happy and he no longer felt needed.

After a year of odd jobs around again came Christmas Eve. All of the reindeer and elves were celebrating in the factory, while Santa and his team were out delivering presents.

All of a sudden Santa called over the loud speaker, "We're coming upon New York City and I can't seem to find the gifts for an entire neighborhood!" After a few frantic minutes, an elf found the misplaced gifts in the back room of the factory. They had been forgotten!

There was no time for Santa to come back and get them. An entire neighborhood of good children would not receive their gifts.

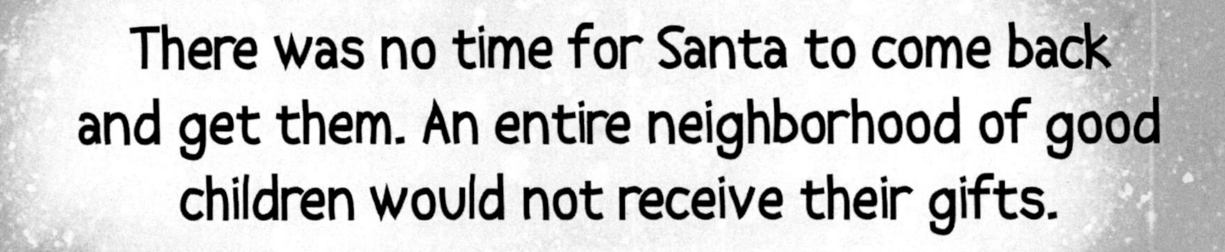

Suddenly, a voice rang out above the sorrowful elves and reindeer, "I can take the gifts!" Sonic stepped forward with a knapsack.

He was the only reindeer strong enough to carry the gifts alone, and the only one fast enough to deliver them on time.

The elves quickly loaded his knapsack with gifts and he bolted off into the night.

Soon, Sonic was flying high above New York City and down into the neighborhood. There he met Santa and the team who received him with cheers.

Sonic gave Santa the knapsack of gifts as he placed them in his big red bag. He had saved the day.

From that Christmas Eve on, Sonic was given his own special job. He would be Santa's Express Reindeer, and rush deliver any and all forgotten gifts to Santa.

He loved his new job and once again felt needed.

Bryan Rucklos is a first time author but lifelong Christmas enthusiast. He has long been enthralled in Christmas and other holiday traditions. Santa's Express Reindeer is a project that had long been in the works but hinged on finding a creative hand that could bring it to life. In his works Bryan hopes that people can rediscover a bit of their childhood and instill a sense of holiday spirit.

Roksolana Panchyshyn is an illustrator that focuses primarily on children's books. In her efforts to bring Sonic to life she fully immersed herself in the Christmas spirit by listening to Christmas music (unseasonably) while creating each illustration. Since her childhood she has always had a deep passion for drawing and has been fortunate enough to live her dream of turning this passion into a profession. She works very closely with her authors to best convey all of the fascination and mystery of the story within her work.

42558587R00015

Made in the USA
San Bernardino, CA
05 December 2016